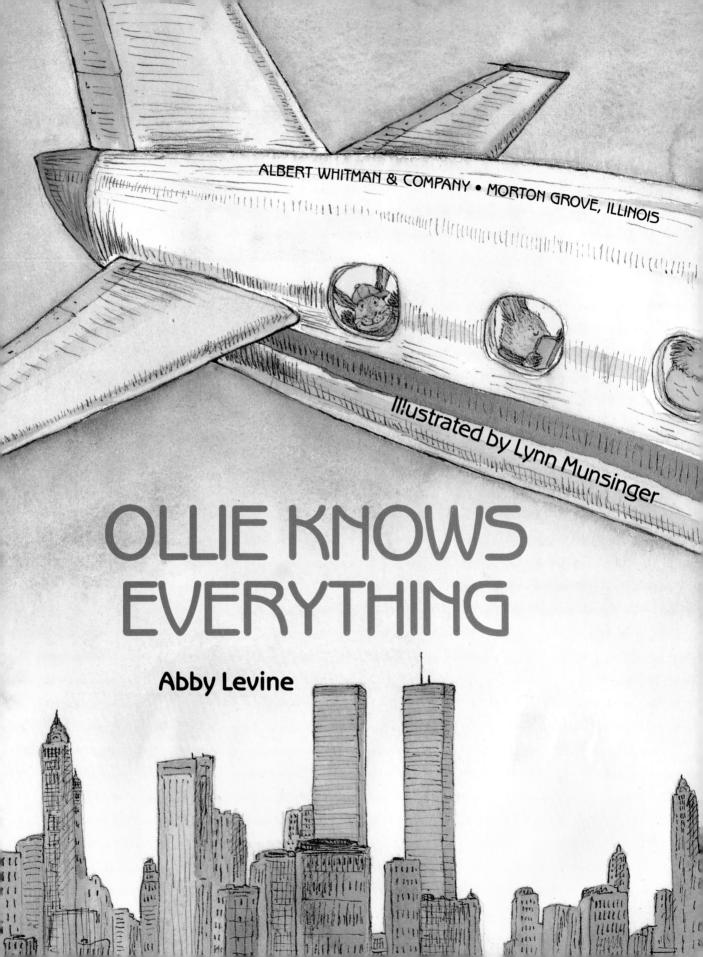

ALBERT WHITMAN & COMPANY • MORTON GROVE, ILLINOIS

Illustrated by Lynn Munsinger

OLLIE KNOWS EVERYTHING

Abby Levine

For Sarah and Susannah,
who are equally wise.
A.L.

For Jack and Julia.
L.M.

Text © 1994 by Abby Levine.
Illustrations © 1994 by Lynn Munsinger.
Cover and interior design by Karen Yops.
The text typeface is Souvenir Light.
Published in 1994 by Albert Whitman & Company,
6340 Oakton Street, Morton Grove, Illinois 60053-2723.
Published simultaneously in Canada
by General Publishing, Limited, Toronto.
Printed in the United States of America.
10 9 8 7 6 5 4 3 2 1

Library of Congress Cataloging-in-Publication Data

Levine, Abby.
Ollie knows everything / Abby Levine;
illustrations by Lynn Munsinger.
p.   cm.
Summary: Herbert's big brother, Ollie, is only two years older,
but he can do everything better, even getting lost.
ISBN 0-8075-6020-0
[1. Rabbits—Fiction.   2. Brothers—Fiction.   3. Lost children—
Fiction.]   I. Munsinger, Lynn, ill.   II. Title.
PZ7.L578201 1994   93-29600
[E]—dc20   CIP   AC

When the O'Hares went to New York, Ollie knew
everything. Just like he did at home.

He knew how to fasten his seatbelt.
He knew how to put the tray down for eating.

When the bags went round, he yelled, "There's our suitcase!"
And it was.

In New York, things were just as bad.

He could read "hamburger" on the menu.
He could open his eyes underwater.

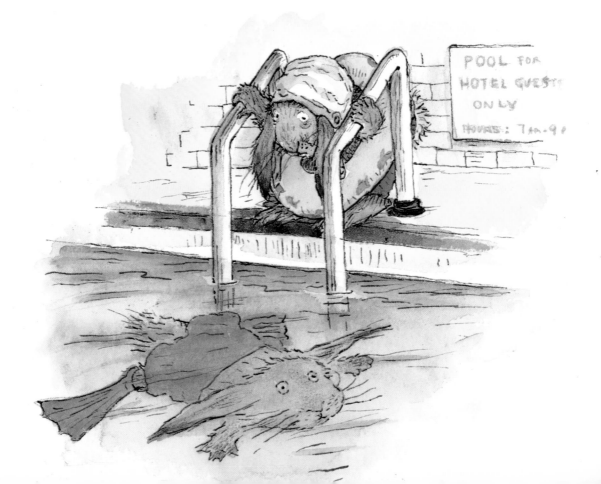

When they went to the top of the Empire State Building,
Ollie pointed to a building nearby. "There's our hotel!"
he shouted.

And it was.

"Ollie always knows everything," Herbert complained
to Mother.

"He doesn't really," Mother said. "But I'm sure it feels
that way."

The streets were noisy and crowded. Everything was
fun to look at. The O'Hares took the subway and the ferry
to Ellis Island.

They saw the Great Hall, where immigrants once came through. Mother said her great-grandmother had stood there, long ago.

Herbert saw a photo of someone who looked like
Mother.
Ollie said they'd learned all about Ellis Island in school.

"Look!" said Herbert when they got back in the subway. "I can put my token in the slot!"

"Big deal!" said Ollie.

"Will he always be older than me," Herbert asked Mother, "even when *I'm* seven?"

"Even when you're both old, gray bunnies, Ollie will still be older," said Mother. She stopped and thought for a little while. "Here's a poem for you," she said.

You were born when he was two.
That's why he knows more than you.
But when you both are big and tall,
Ollie won't know more at all!

"Did you make that up?" Herbert asked.

"Just now, just for you," said Mother.

But Herbert was not cheered. It would be years until he and Ollie were both grown up.

The subway was crammed with riders, and the O'Hares
all had to stand. The speeding train lurched back and

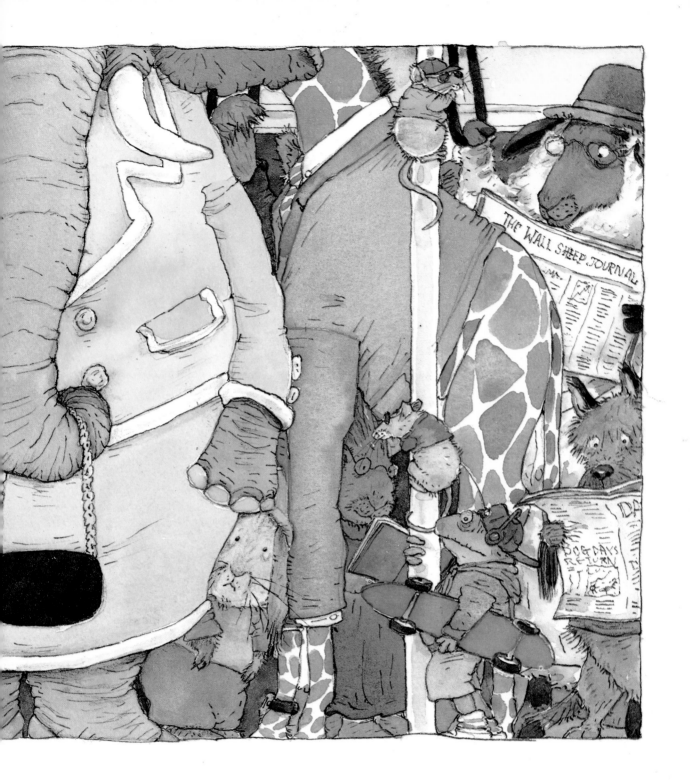

forth. Herbert felt squooshed. Ollie was stuck between a
large lady and a tall, thin man.

The train pulled into the station. "Time to get off!"
said Father. They were swept away in a throng of passengers.

"Ollie . . . ," Father began, but there was no answer.
Ollie was not there!

The doors snapped shut.

Herbert turned around. "Ollie's still in the train!" he yelled.

As the train sped off, they could see Ollie's face pressed against the window. Then the train disappeared into the darkness.

"I'll take the next train to the next station and look!" Father shouted. "Maybe Ollie got off and is waiting for us there!"

"I'll find the police station!" Mother shouted back. And she ran up the stairs, pulling Herbert by one paw.

The police were very kind. "Not to worry, Ma'am,"
said Sergeant Wolf. "We'll find your lad." He took Ollie's
description. Then he talked on the phone to the subway
police. "He's seven years old, and he's wearing a red
T-shirt, blue shorts, and an orange baseball cap. He
answers to the name of 'Ollie.'"

Herbert wished he could be lost, too. Ollie always did
everything better.

After a long wait, they saw Father trudge into the station. "I didn't see Ollie anywhere," he said grimly.

"Go back to your hotel," said Sergeant Wolf. "We'll be in touch with you there."

Mother and Father walked slowly back to the hotel. They each held tightly to one of Herbert's paws.

"Can I be the oldest now?" he asked. "Can I be the one to tell his teacher?"

But neither Mother nor Father replied.

Suddenly Herbert remembered how Ollie had looked with his face up against the window. Ollie had been scared! What if he was scared now, somewhere all by himself?

Herbert's heart beat very fast. "Do you think Ollie will come back?" he asked.

"He'll be okay," said Mother. But tears were streaming down her cheeks.

"I'm sure he will," said Father. But Father did not look sure at all.

The streets were noisy and crowded. Everything looked sad and scary.

They entered the hotel lobby—and there was Ollie! He
was sitting at the bellhop's counter, holding a lollipop.
There was a small crowd of people around him, and a

policewoman, too. Ollie was talking excitedly to everyone.
"Ollie!" yelled Mother and Father. They grabbed Ollie
and hugged him. "How did you get here?" Father asked.

"I got off at the next stop with everyone else," Ollie explained. "I followed them all upstairs. Then I saw the Empire State Building. I knew our hotel was nearby, so I just walked back here."

"I'm amazed!" said Mother.

"I'm flabbergasted!" said Father.

"Smart kid," said the bellhop.

"Brave boy," said the policewoman, who had a gun in
her holster and handcuffs on her belt.

Herbert's mouth dropped open. It was true. Ollie *did*
know everything.

Afterwards, the O'Hares rested in their hotel room.
Herbert and Ollie raced their cars on the carpet while
Mother and Father watched "Paws" on television.
Herbert's cars won twice. The air conditioner hummed,
and the room was cozy.

"Were you scared in the train?" Herbert whispered.

Ollie didn't answer right away. Then he said softly,
"Maybe a little."

They raced their cars a little more.

"Mother, make up a poem for Ollie," said Herbert.
Mother thought for a moment. Then she said,

> *Ollie rode off underground.*
> *He got lost and then got found.*

"I found myself," Ollie pointed out.

"You sure did!" said Father, giving each boy a big squeeze.

"Come on," Ollie said to Herbert. "Let's all go down to the pool. I'll teach you how to open your eyes underwater."

Ollie and Herbert swam all evening. They searched underwater for sharks and enemy submarines, and Ollie taught Herbert the bunny paddle.

Mother smiled at them. "Oh," she said. "It's so good to have Ollie back."

And it was.